The DINOSAURS
A New Discovery

Author
Janet Stewart

Illustration & Design
Chris Walker

Editor
Norman Shrive

CHP BOOKS

Cyril Hayes Press Inc.
3312 Mainway, Burlington, Ontario L7M 1A7
One Colomba Drive, Niagara Falls,
New York 14305

ABOUT THIS BOOK

This book will take you on a long journey through the past to a time when dinosaurs roamed the earth. You will meet ferocious Tyrannosaurus rex and his cousin Albertosaurus. You will also get to know other dinosaurs like Diplodocus, Stegosaurus and Apatosaurus, which was once known as Brontosaurus.

Traveling the globe, we will see where the dinosaurs were found and how they were preserved. You can organize a dinosaur hunt and unearth your own secrets of the past.

Then we'll enter the mysterious realm of the disappearance of the dinosaurs. Why, after ruling the earth for 140 million years, did they become extinct? Whatever caused the disappearance of the dinosaurs could repeat itself in the future. As we learn about their destruction, we may discover the clues to avoiding our own.

CONTENTS

IGUANODON

OUR MYSTERIOUS PAST

Man's curiosity is endless! Through the centuries, we have searched for answers to questions like: Where did we come from? How long have we been here? Who are our ancestors? and on and on. Science - the study of knowledge - has helped us understand some of the mysteries of our past.

One field of science, archaeology, studies man, and the preserved remains of his past life. Another field, geology, looks at changes in the earth by close examination of rock and soil. These two sciences give archaeologists and geologists information about past times.

For us, time means things like "time to go to school" or "time to eat." For these scientists, questions of time refer to the age of the earth and, in the case of dinosaurs, the age of fossil remains. While our clock is seconds, minutes, hours, days and years, scientists think in terms of eras covering millions of years.

The chart below gives some idea of the different stages of the earth's history, from its beginnings up to the appearance of man.

HOW OLD IS THE EARTH?

It's almost impossible to imagine the exact age of the earth or how it began. While you and I and the rest of mankind have been around for only a few million years, other forms of life, like marine algae, and small animals with no backbones (invertebrates), have been on earth for almost a billion years. Geologists and archaeologists study the different rocks, soils and fossils found in the ground and use them to determine the age of the earth. Some scientists believe that the earth is at least four and one-half billion years old.

ARCHEOZOIC
(THREE BILLION YEARS AGO)

PROTEROZOIC
(ONE BILLION YEARS AGO)

BEGINNINGS OF LIFE

INVERTEBRATES AND
MARINE ALGAE

PALEOZOIC
(SIX HUNDRED MILLION YEARS AGO)

THE AGE OF TERRIBLE LIZARDS

A science, closely tied in with geology and archaeology, developed in the 1800s. Charles Lyell called it "paleontology," the "science of ancient being." Paleontologists use fossils and rocks to study past life. It was these explorers of time who first identified the remains of the "terrible lizards" that once ruled the earth - the DINOSAURS!

A DINOSAUR TIME CLOCK

While our time clock can be traced back as far as three or four million years, the dinosaur time clock covers over two hundred million years. Through this time period, called the "Mesozoic," hundreds of different dinosaurs lived all over the earth.

Did You Know?

This Hadrosaur breathed through tubes that went through the crest from its nostrils and to the back of its throat.

FISH, AMPHIBIANS,REPTILES, FERNS, CYCADS, CONIFERS

MESOZOIC (TWO HUNDRED MILLION YEARS AGO)

DINOSAURS, MAMMALS, BIRDS, FLOWERING PLANTS,GRASSES

CENOZOIC (SIXTY-FIVE MILLION YEARS AGO)

MAN .

LIFE'S BEGINNINGS

Life on earth first began in the seas, with proteins and cells. Proteins are chemicals scientists think were formed from sunlight and gases. Tiny cells fed on these proteins and, over hundreds of years, developed or evolved into the first plants - marine algae.

These plants gave off oxygen into the atmosphere. One-celled animals developed and ate them. Over the years, larger animals like worms, jellyfish and other invertebrates evolved from these cells.

Then creatures with backbones (vertebrates) developed, at first in the form of jawless fish. Jawed fish of two types, the ray fin and the lobe fin, emerged years later. Most of our fish today evolved from the ray fins. Lobe fin fish still exist today, but are very rare. It is believed that the earliest amphibians – animals that could survive on land, but had to return to water to lay eggs – evolved gradually from the lobe fins.

These ancient amphibians had strong, stumpy fins that helped them to drag their large bodies across land. Over time, reptiles, capable of laying their eggs on land, developed from these amphibians. These eggs are known as amniote eggs. The development of the amniote eggs meant that the reptiles were no longer tied to the water and could travel farther inland.

From these reptiles evolved various different groups. One of these, the thecodonts, looked very much like our present-day crocodiles, but they had big tusks and were as long as a bus! From them came a species that we now call dinosaurs.

There was an incredible variety of different kinds of dinosaurs, but the main division is between the saurischia (with a reptile-like pelvis) and the ornithischia (with a bird-like pelvis).

What the world was like then...

Scientists believe that two hundred million years ago (the Triassic period, which is the first part of the Mesozoic era) our seven continents were joined together and formed one gigantic landmass that they call Pangaea. Creatures alive at that time could travel back and forth, migrate, for example, over the super continent.

If we had been alive then, we would not have had to cross the sea to visit other countries; all our maps would be different and so would the way we live. But over time Pangaea began to break up. Europe, Asia and North America moved north, while Australia, Antarctica, South America and Africa moved in the opposite direction, until, over millions of years, the landmasses of the world reached the positions they have today. Even today the continents under our feet are moving slightly.

Did you know that North America is shifting away from Europe at the rate of 2 cm (almost an inch) every year?

As this movement was taking place, the prehistoric creatures migrating over land eventually could not reach their usual feeding and nesting places. As a result, some species disappeared, while others were able to adapt to their new environments.

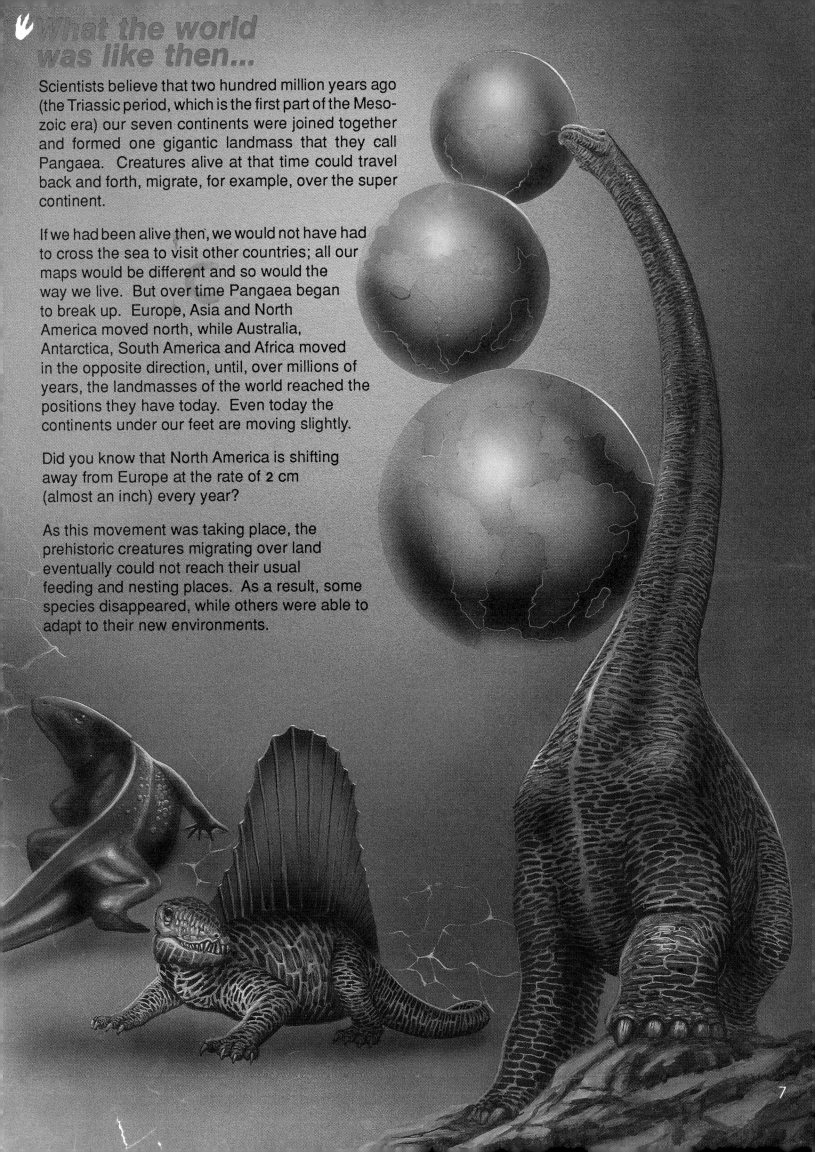

A DIFFERENT WORLD

When the dinosaurs first began to rule the earth, the land was mainly the browns and greens of trees and ferns. There were no brightly colored flowers, only the blue sky and blue-green sea for variety. As water invaded the landmass, more vegetation evolved, but the world still lacked the bright colors of today.

WARMTH ALL YEAR ROUND

About one hundred million years ago (the latter third, or Cretaceous part, of the Mesozoic era), the world began to be a bright, beautiful place as the first plants and flowers, with their reds, yellows and purples, appeared. Great creatures roamed the land, huge flying creatures called Pterosaurs ruled the skies, and a variety of smaller creatures populated the earth and seas.

During that time so long ago, the world was much warmer than it is now. Tropical temperatures all year round caused plants and trees to grow quickly. Scientists believe that even the poles were free of ice and snow. The dinosaurs lived in a world that gave them everything they needed to flourish.

1. Dead dinosaur on river bank

2. Flesh rots away, leaving exposed bones

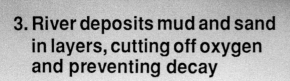

3. River deposits mud and sand in layers, cutting off oxygen and preventing decay

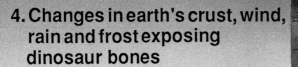

4. Changes in earth's crust, wind, rain and frost exposing dinosaur bones

FOSSIL DETECTIVES

The mysteries of dinosaurs and of other past life can be partly solved by examination of fossils. Fossils are preserved remains of plants and animals that may have died millions of years ago.

Imagine putting together a puzzle, without any reference to what it should look like, and not even knowing if you have all the pieces. This is what it's like putting together dinosaur fossils. Almost everyone has heard of a Brontosaurus, the giant plant-eating dinosaur. In actual fact, the skeleton that was named Brontosaurus was parts of two different dinosaurs. The skeleton was of a dinosaur now named Apatasaurus, but when scientists assembled it, they used a skull and front legs from a different dinosaur called Camarasaurus. This mistake was only discovered in the 1970s; the correct pieces were substituted, and the mystery of the Apatasaurus was finally revealed.

TRACE FOSSILS and IMPRESSIONS

These fossils of footprints, burrows, skin or leaves, give paleontologists information about the range and type of movement of dinosaurs. The Apatasaurus (Brontosaurus) was thought to have spent most of its time in water, to help support its huge body, and if it had walked on land, that it would have had to drag its huge tail behind it. Trace fossils have revealed that the Apatasaurus not only walked on land, but, because there are footprints and no tail drag marks, it must have held its tail up when walking.

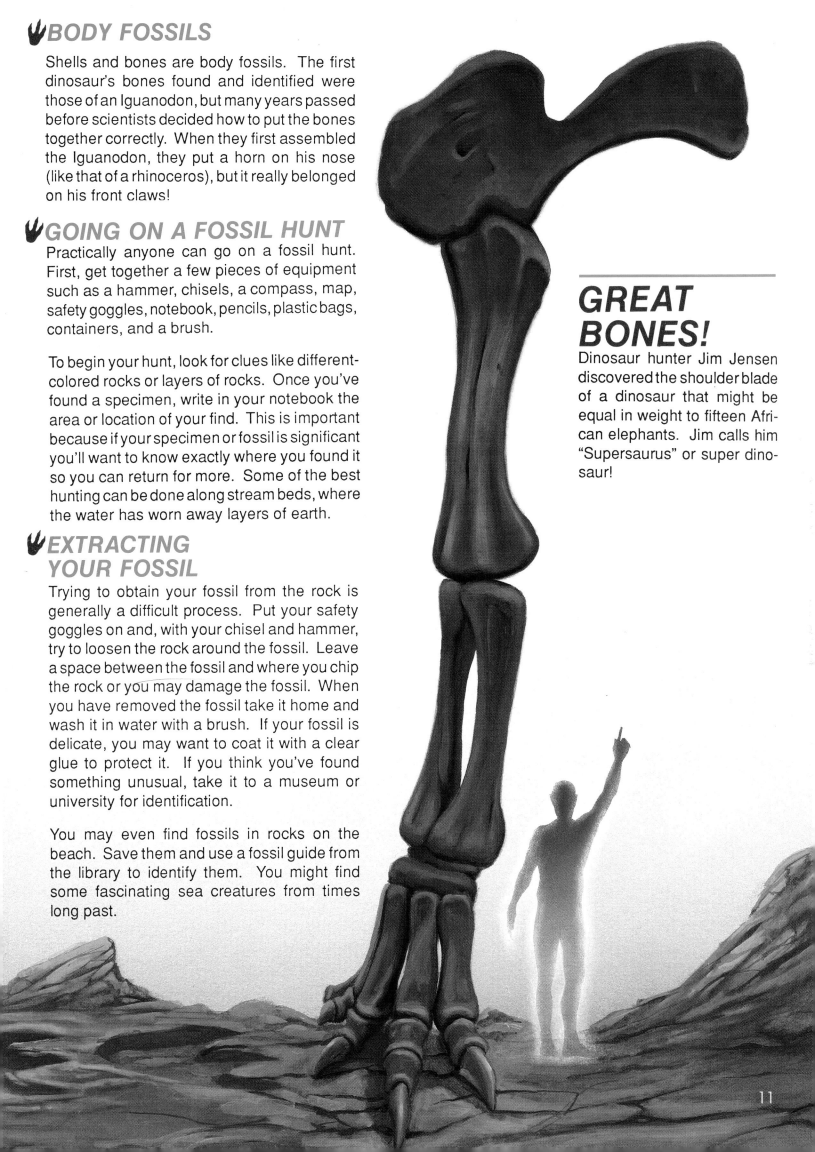

BODY FOSSILS

Shells and bones are body fossils. The first dinosaur's bones found and identified were those of an Iguanodon, but many years passed before scientists decided how to put the bones together correctly. When they first assembled the Iguanodon, they put a horn on his nose (like that of a rhinoceros), but it really belonged on his front claws!

GOING ON A FOSSIL HUNT

Practically anyone can go on a fossil hunt. First, get together a few pieces of equipment such as a hammer, chisels, a compass, map, safety goggles, notebook, pencils, plastic bags, containers, and a brush.

To begin your hunt, look for clues like different-colored rocks or layers of rocks. Once you've found a specimen, write in your notebook the area or location of your find. This is important because if your specimen or fossil is significant you'll want to know exactly where you found it so you can return for more. Some of the best hunting can be done along stream beds, where the water has worn away layers of earth.

EXTRACTING YOUR FOSSIL

Trying to obtain your fossil from the rock is generally a difficult process. Put your safety goggles on and, with your chisel and hammer, try to loosen the rock around the fossil. Leave a space between the fossil and where you chip the rock or you may damage the fossil. When you have removed the fossil take it home and wash it in water with a brush. If your fossil is delicate, you may want to coat it with a clear glue to protect it. If you think you've found something unusual, take it to a museum or university for identification.

You may even find fossils in rocks on the beach. Save them and use a fossil guide from the library to identify them. You might find some fascinating sea creatures from times long past.

GREAT BONES!

Dinosaur hunter Jim Jensen discovered the shoulder blade of a dinosaur that might be equal in weight to fifteen African elephants. Jim calls him "Supersaurus" or super dinosaur!

DATING THE DINOSAUR

It's not easy to imagine anything that's millions of years old. Most of the things we know are old in terms of days, years and centuries. We've seen how fossils are made, but how do we know how old they are? Scientists use a variety of methods to measure the age of rocks and fossils.

Carbon 14

Measuring the amount of carbon 14 in fossils can show how old they are. But, because carbon 14 breaks down after only a few thousand years, it isn't useful for dating dinosaur bones.

Radiometric dating

Using complex machines, scientists study the mineral and chemical contents of rocks and fossils. Some of these substances are radioactive (emit rays) and can be measured with equipment like a radiometer. Certain changes in the substances indicate a particular period of time has gone by, and the rock or fossil can be dated accordingly.

Two methods are frequently used when dating rocks and fossils from the dinosaur's time.

Potassium-argon method

Potassium in rocks changes over time and produces argon. Radiometric equipment measures the amount of argon and potassium in the rock and uses the ratio of the two to determine its general age.

Uranium-lead method

In a similar manner, uranium in a rock breaks down over time and changes to lead. By measuring the amount of uranium and lead in a rock, scientists can determine the age of the rock.

ᨕ Stratigraphical Paleontology

Related to these methods is the study of the layers of rock and the fossils within them. This is called stratigraphical paleontology and gives a fairly accurate age of rocks and fossils. This method looks at the bottom layers of sediment (rock, sand and clay) as older than the top layers. Picking out fossils of animals found only in a particular layer, scientists form "index fossils." These markers of time are used to tell the age of the rocks. Index markers from the dinosaur's era are echinoderms, ammonites and bivalves (all are small sea creatures). Using these methods, scientists are able to date the planet earth, and the animals and plants that lived there.

MESOZOIC ERA

Late Cretaceous

Echinoderm

Middle Jurassic

Ammonite

Early Triassic

Bivalve

THECODONTS

ORNITHISCHIAN DINOSAURS

SAURISCHIAN DINOSAURS

THE DINOSAUR ORDER

Over 340 genera, i.e. groups of closely related species, of dinosaurs have been identified from fossils. As we have seen, the evolutionary process began with the lobe fins. Then came the amphibians, and later the the reptiles, some of whom developed the capability of laying amniote eggs on land. From these came the thecodonts, which, in turn, evolved into the two main divisions of dinosaurs. These two divisions are referred to as the Saurischian order and the Ornithischian order.

To complicate matters slightly, while this dinosaur evolution was taking place, other groups of creatures not classified as dinosaurs were evolving. The crocodilians and the birds have survived from the Triassic period until the present. The Pterosaurs - flying reptiles - lived from the Jurassic to the Cretaceous period. Some scientists now believe that the two dinosaur orders should combine with the birds to form a separate class from the reptiles and be called Dinosauria.

BRACHIOSAURUS

THE SAURISCHIAN FAMILY

These were characterized by their lizard-like hip bones. The three main hip bones were arranged like those of most reptiles. They had pointed teeth extending right around their jaws.

Two main groups of Saurischians evolved: The theropods or "beast feet" were two-legged (bipedal) carnivores (meat eaters) and the sauropods or '"lizard feet" were four-legged (quadrupedal) mainly herbivores (plant eaters).

TYRANNOSAURUS REX

ILIUM

ISCHIUM

PUBIS

THE ORNITHISCHIAN FAMILY

These had bird-like hip bones and, eventually, a bird-like bill that probably replaced previous front teeth.

Several groups of dinosaurs evolved from the Ornithischians. One was the ornithopods, or "bird feet" with two legs; another was the plated, horned and armored group that walked on all four legs.

STEGOSAURUS

ILIUM

ISCHIUM

PUBIS

MEAT EATERS AND PLANT EATERS

Both orders of dinosaurs had carnivores and herbivores. Among the former were armored varieties like Stegosaurus, and in the latter were some of the larger dinosaurs like Brachiosaurus and Diplodocus.

15

Includes the better-known dinosaurs like Tyrannosaurus and Apatasaurus. There was a great range of size in this group, some being longer than a bus, others as small as your foot.

1. Deinonychus

Named for its "terrible claws," Deinonychus was one of the fastest and fiercest of the dinosaurs. One claw on the second toe was about the size of your entire hand! It could easily injure dinosaurs much bigger than itself.

2. Allosaurus

Allosaurids lived on every continent; these carnivorous monsters were heavily built and probably could not move very fast. It has been suggested that they may have hunted in packs to bring down huge prey like the Apatasaurus.

3. Brachiosaurus

Until recently, Brachiosaurus was thought to be the largest dinosaur. Scientists think that this dinosaur weighed as much as a blue whale, or as much as 120 tons!

SAURISCHIAN

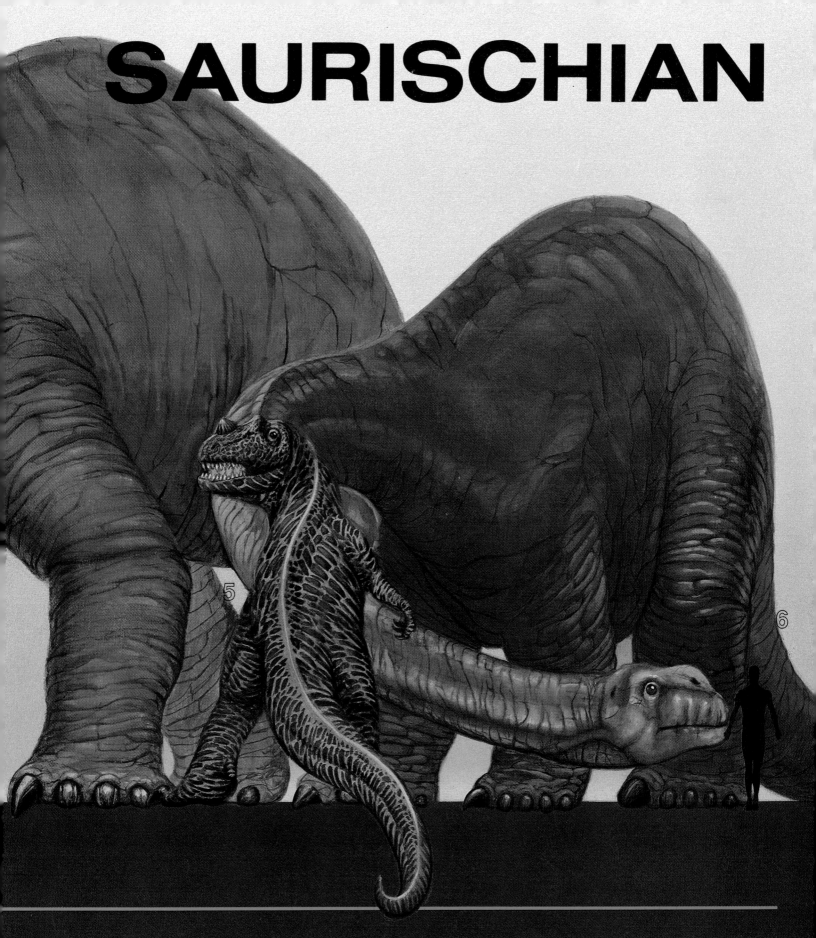

4. Tyrannosaurus
The "tyrant lizard" Tyrannosaurus was one of the fiercest of dinosaurs. A carnivore with more than sixty razor-sharp teeth, mighty Tyrannosaurus probably terrorized most other dinosaurs.

5. Ceratosaurus
You wouldn't want to get a Ceratosaurus angry! It had a horn on its nose that must have been a very effective weapon indeed.

6. Apatasaurus
This immense Saurischian grew to about seventy feet in length. Judging from its size it must have eaten almost continuously. Apatasaurus swallowed whole plants, which were ground up in its stomach by pebbles that it had swallowed.

Duckbills, boneheads, horned, plated and spiked dinosaurs made up the Ornithischian order. Many of these dinosaurs were so well protected that they could fight off even Tyrannosaurus rex - the killer carnivore!

1 Iguandon

Traveling in herds, Iguandons probably used their spiked thumbs to dig up food or to protect themselves.

2 Triceratops

Many different kinds of Triceratops have been found. Each had two horns longer than your arm on their brows and a shorter one above the nose. Not a dinosaur you'd want to rub noses with!

ORNITHISCHIAN

3 Hadrosaurus

Broad, toothless beaks and crested heads gave Hadrosaurus the nickname "duckbill." Like chipmunks, duckbills could store unchewed food in their bulging cheeks, while using teeth in their jaws to chew.

4 Stegosaurus

Stegosaurus was a large, heavy dinosaur with plates down its back. The biggest plate was probably about the size of an average window. On the Stegosaurus's tail were at least four spikes that could fatally wound an enemy.

5 Euoplocephalus

This dinosaur was covered in armor from the tip of its tail to the top of its head. Euoplocephalus had shields, plates, spines and a club tail to keep away his enemies.

19

DINOSAUR MYTHS

Mysteries of the dinosaurs: Were they cold-blooded, warm-blooded, land dwelling? Did they have one brain or two? Were they all green? The questions are endless. We'll never know the complete truth about the dinosaurs because so many secrets died with them. But scientists are uncovering more and more facts about the dinosaurs as they discover more and more fossil remains.

GIANTS

Sauropod dinosaurs, like Diplodocus, were quadropeds (walked on all four legs). Dinosaurs like Tyrannosaurus were bipeds (walked on two legs). Many bipeds used their front legs or forelimbs much as we use our arms. They could hold food or fight off attackers with their claws. When sauropods were first discovered, it was thought that they were too big and too heavy to walk on land. Most believed that dinosaurs like Brachiosaurus must have lived in lakes and rivers where the water's buoyancy would have held them up. However, recent findings of trackways seem to indicate they were quite capable of traveling on land.

A DINOSAUR BRAIN

Compared to the size of their bodies, the brains of most dinosaurs were small. But many scientists believe that dinosaurs developed very good senses of smell, sight and hearing, compensating for a lack of general intelligence. Some dinosaurs may have been able to communicate by making sounds.

General intelligence is measured by an "encephalization quotient" - a ratio of brain weight to body weight. By the latter part of the Mesozoic Era, a few of the smaller dinosaurs had developed a ratio that was almost the same as that of

the early mammals. Paleontologist Dale Russell thinks that if dinosaurs hadn't become extinct, they would have developed into creatures with a quotient not much lower than that of humans.

ONE BRAIN OR TWO?

A Stegosaurus was found to have what looked like two brains. Where his spine crossed the pelvic bone there was an area for another brain, many times the size of the one in the skull. It turns out that it's not really another brain, but a control center for the tail and hind legs. This center helped the dinosaur use his tail and legs more quickly than if signals had been sent from the skull all the way to the end of the tail - more than nine meters (thirty feet) long!

ECTOTHERMS AND ENDOTHERMS

When you hear the word 'warm-blooded,' you probably think of warm blood rushing through veins. And 'cold-blooded' brings to mind those slimy reptiles who probably have icy blue blood in their veins. This isn't quite right. Actually, the words 'cold-blooded' and 'warm-blooded' are deceiving since they don't refer to temperature of the blood itself.

Cold-blooded animals, like reptiles, are called ectotherms, and absorb heat from the sun to warm their bodies. Once heated up, they can begin a day of activity - mainly a day of finding food. At night when it's cooler, their body temperature drops, and most remain stationary and inactive.

Mammals are warm-blooded and are called endotherms. They maintain a constant body temperature during the day and at night. Outside environmental changes in temperatures don't affect their internal body temperatures.

Poikilotherms are animals like fish that have no control over their internal body temperatures. Many of these animals experience a wide variety of temperature changes, depending on their environment.

Because dinosaurs are from the Reptilia class, many assume they are ectotherms. However, some dinosaurs like Deinonychus and Compsognathus were built in ways similar to modern-day birds, which are endothermic.

EGGS OR BABIES?

Most dinosaurs laid eggs, and large nests of hatched and unhatched eggs have been found. However, some scientists think that Apatasaurus had live babies that weighed more than a full-grown pig!

THE MYTHS CONTINUE

When dinosaurs were first discovered, they were thought to be slow, sluggish beasts with brutish manners that left their young to fend for themselves, much like many modern reptiles. As more was learned from fossils, particularly trace fossils of Hadrosaur footprints found in the United States, it was learned that some species traveled in herds or packs, possibly keeping younger members in the center to protect them.

When dinosaurs laid eggs, some of them probably stayed close to the nest and took care of the young until they could move off by themselves.

HADROSAURUS

COMPSOGNATHUS

Compsognathus was a small dinosaur that looked like a bird. He may have been a scavenger - eating dinosaur eggs whenever he could steal them!

ARCHAEOPTERYX

QUETZALCOATLUS

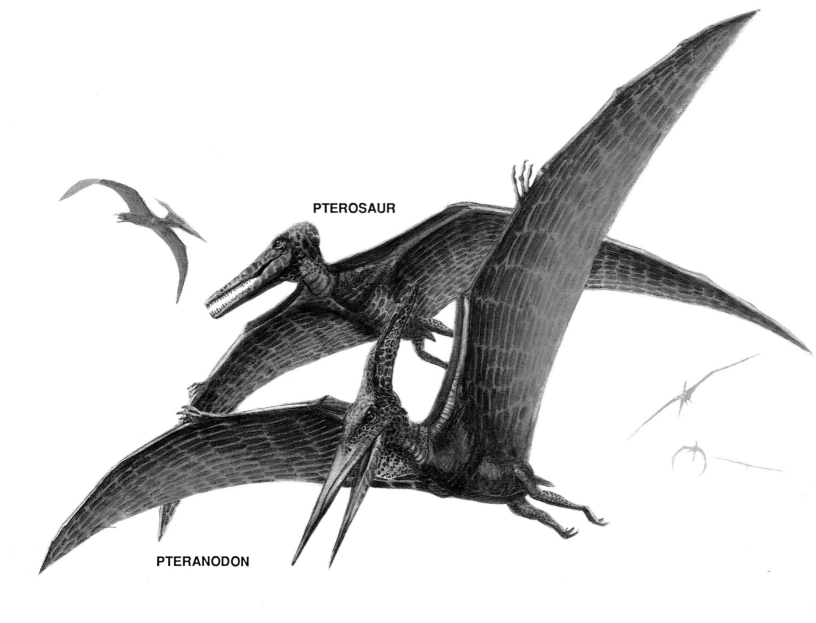

PTEROSAUR

PTERANODON

Are Birds Really Related to Dinosaurs?

Most of us know who our ancestors are. We can trace our family back through time and discover generations of relatives. And our descendants will be able to do the same. Paleontologists try to determine family lines of dinosaurs. Scientists have tried to find out if dinosaurs left any descendants alive when they became extinct sixty-five million years ago. Did they find any?

A few of them believe that our modern-day birds are the only living relatives of the dinosaurs. Birds have an ancestor from the Archosauria superorder common to the dinosaurs - the thecodonts. The discovery of Archaeopteryx, a feathered type of dinosaur much like the small Compsognathus, caused some researchers to link this particular dinosaur to birds. While this dinosaur had feathered wings, it also had features like sharp teeth more typical of dinosaurs. Scientists continue to argue about this, and a few can't look at a bird without wondering if it is really the last of those great ruling reptiles!

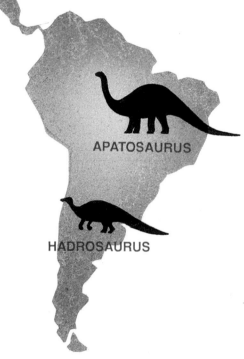

A WORLD OF
DISCOVERY

Fossil hunters around the world have made amazing discoveries of dinosaur bones, eggs and trackways. From lands like those in Alberta, Canada, that were once swampy, warm plains, these hunters have unearthed mysteries of the past. The most extensive discoveries have been made in Alberta, Montana and Mongolia.

North American finds included Coelophysis, Anchisaurus, Allosaurus, Diplodocus, Stegosaurus, Tyrannosaurus, Parasaurolophus and Tricertops. The Badlands of Alberta have been a gold mine, and future explorations will only yield more.

Exciting discoveries have been made in South America's Brazil and Argentina. Sauropods and duckbills, previously not known in these areas, have been found. Some of the earliest dinosaurs are from these regions.

Alaskan dinosaur finds of Hadrosaurs and Tyrannosaurus types in 1985 are another indication that dinosaurs roamed over the entire globe. Previously, they hadn't been found as far north.

A wide variety of bones has been found in Africa. Brachiosaurus, Syntarsus, Spinosaurus and many of the smaller dinosaurs have been found there. Most have been dug up in Tanzania.

The 1980s have revealed many Australian and New Zealand finds. Sauropod and Ornithischian bipedal dinosaur finds have made Australia a hot spot for future dinosaur discoveries.

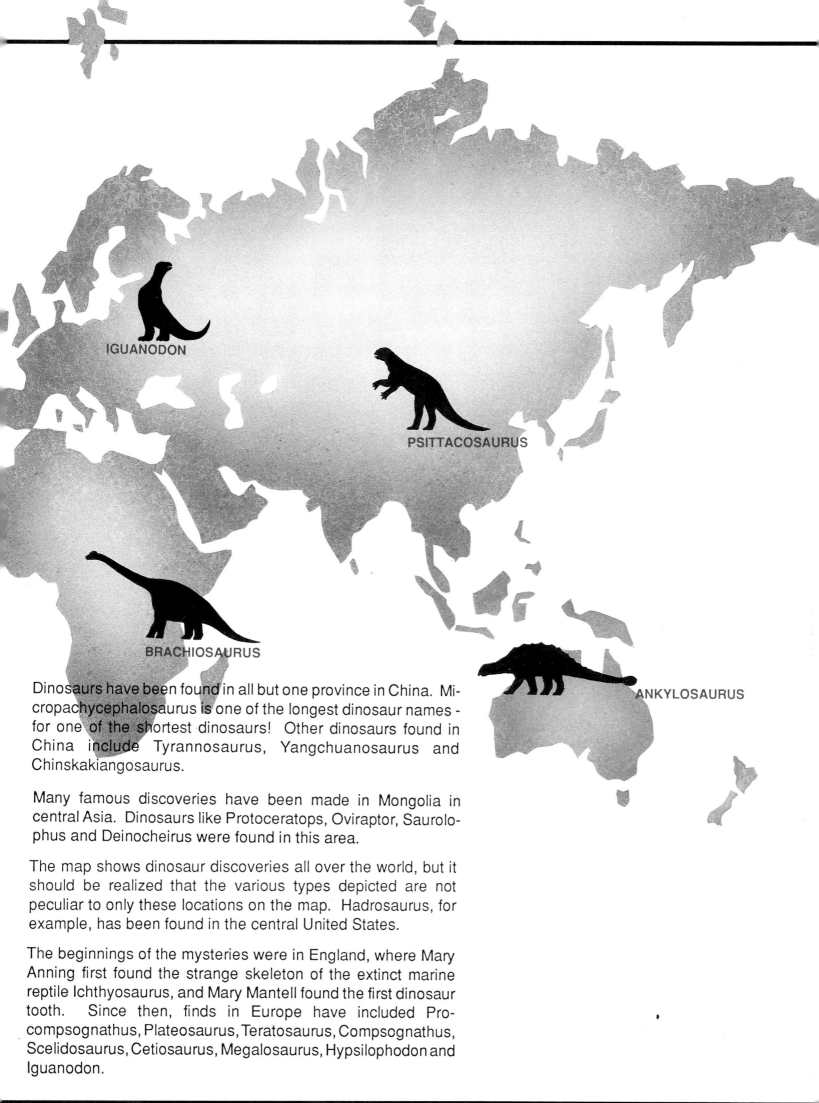

IGUANODON

PSITTACOSAURUS

BRACHIOSAURUS

ANKYLOSAURUS

Dinosaurs have been found in all but one province in China. Micropachycephalosaurus is one of the longest dinosaur names - for one of the shortest dinosaurs! Other dinosaurs found in China include Tyrannosaurus, Yangchuanosaurus and Chinskakiangosaurus.

Many famous discoveries have been made in Mongolia in central Asia. Dinosaurs like Protoceratops, Oviraptor, Saurolophus and Deinocheirus were found in this area.

The map shows dinosaur discoveries all over the world, but it should be realized that the various types depicted are not peculiar to only these locations on the map. Hadrosaurus, for example, has been found in the central United States.

The beginnings of the mysteries were in England, where Mary Anning first found the strange skeleton of the extinct marine reptile Ichthyosaurus, and Mary Mantell found the first dinosaur tooth. Since then, finds in Europe have included Procompsognathus, Plateosaurus, Teratosaurus, Compsognathus, Scelidosaurus, Cetiosaurus, Megalosaurus, Hypsilophodon and Iguanodon.

GETTING CLOSE TO A
DINOSAUR

Books such as this one can tell all we know about dinosaurs, but to really appreciate their wonder and grandeur we should actually see and perhaps even touch them. Dinosaurs are public property and may be viewed and examined in parks and museums all over the world.

One important site is the Tyrrell Museum of Paleontology in Drumheller, Alberta, Canada. To wander through this remarkable place is to pass three billion years of life on earth and to see the greatest collection of dinosaur skeletons in the world. Surrounded by eroded, sun-baked valleys and canyons in the Badlands of Alberta, their mystery is preserved for all of us to marvel at. What until only recently was called the "Great American Desert," sixty-five million years ago was a lush, swampy home for many kinds of dinosaurs.

As we walk through the past we will see the ferocious Albertosaurus. Then his cousin, Tyrannosaurus rex, the biggest carnivore (meat eater) ever to roam the earth.

Over there is Erlickosaurus, not much taller than a full-grown man, a dinosaur that probably swam and hunted for fish.

And there is one of the Hadrosaur family, looking like a large kangaroo, an eater of plants and trees. Or Triceratop, with his impressive spikes.

There are also Ichthyosaurs, Plesiosaurs, and Placodonts. Even a Pterosaur, a strange, hollow-boned reptile that was probably the first flying vertebrate.

All in all, there are over fifty species of dinosaurs at the Tyrrell, a truly fascinating collection!

TYRANNOSAURUS REX

WHERE DID ALL THE DINOSAURS GO?

Ever since the early 1800s, when the first dinosaur bones were discovered, people have asked "What happened to the dinosaurs?" Sixty-five million years ago, after ruling the entire globe for over 150 million years, the dinosaurs became extinct! Why?

What does it mean to be "extinct?" At various times throughout earth's history, groups of animals have completely disappeared. These species die out because they can't cope with changes in the environment. Sometimes these changes are natural catastrophes or disasters, like earthquakes or floods. An example of an extinction more recent than that of the dinosaurs was the disappearance of the mastodons and mammoths.

A mastodon is a large, extinct animal similar to an elephant, but larger. A mammoth is an extinct elephant with hairy skin and long, curving tusks.

🐾 THE EARTH'S HISTORY OF EXTINCTIONS

Fossils in the earth show that forms of life have been destroyed at certain times over the past five hundred million years. Sometimes there is a sudden change in the kinds of fossils in the layers of rock. For example, after the dinosaurs disappeared sixty-five million years ago, no fossils appeared in the rocks. Then, in the next level of rock, fossils of different species appeared. Between the layers of rock, a red clay-like substance was found. After closely examining the layer, scientists discovered that it contained high concentrations of iridium - a substance usually found in the earth's core. This information provided evidence that a change had occurred on earth about sixty-five million years ago. The dinosaurs were just one of the many species that couldn't cope with the change.

Using the evidence from the fossils and layers of rock, we can chart extinctions of animals over the history of the earth. Trilobites disappeared over 240 million years ago during the greatest mass extinction ever when almost 96% of all species living in the oceans were destroyed. At that time, most life on earth was in the oceans. Placodonts died out about 215 million years ago, and sea creatures like ammonites died about 140 million years ago. Perhaps the most talked about extinction occurred sixty-five million years ago with the disappearance of the dinosaurs.

Mastodons
TEN THOUSAND YEARS AGO

Dinosaurs
65 MILLION YEARS AGO

Ammonites
140 MILLION YEARS AGO

Placodonts
215 MILLION YEARS AGO

Trilobites
240 MILLION YEARS AGO

EXTINCTION THEORIES

We know the dinosaurs disappeared or became extinct, but we still don't know why. Everyone seems to have a theory or a reason for their disappearance. A once popular theory was that the mammals and mammal-like reptiles living during the Mesozoic era tricked the dinosaurs and ate all their eggs. No new dinosaurs were born and the old ones died. This theory isn't very convincing to most of us. Dinosaurs were capable of surviving for over 140 million years. It seems unlikely that mammals would be able to destroy them so suddenly and completely.

Until recently, the most widely accepted theory blamed the death of the dinosaurs on "climatic cooling." This theory claimed that temperature changes around the world forced the dinosaurs farther south. Ultimately, changes in the environment led to the death of all the dinosaurs as they tried to cope with a changing world, and failed.

Today, however, scientists are looking to the stars to explain the extinction of the "ruling reptiles."

Comets, Asteroids and Meteorites

Comets are described as "dirty snowballs," made up of ice, rock and gases. They have long tails that point away from the sun as they orbit or circle it.

Asteroids are rocky objects orbiting in space between Mars and Jupiter - planets in our solar system. Some are as small as a boulder, others as big as a house. The biggest one has a diameter of nearly five hundred miles!

Meteorites are small particles of rock and/or iron that have landed on earth. In space they are called meteors.

Death by a Greek Goddess

A theory called Nemesis, after the Greek goddess who punished the proud — in this case, the dinosaurs — claims that a "Death Star" caused havoc in the galaxy above the earth as it passed through the so-called "Oort Cloud" and sent comets on a crash course toward the earth. The Oort Cloud is an area in space believed to contain billions of comets that travel around the sun in their orbit.

Once the meteors crashed on earth, the atmosphere was filled with billions of particles that blocked the sun's rays. Plants died and temperatures dropped drastically. Species that couldn't adjust - died. One of these was the dinosaur.

The Terror of Planet X

A theory similar to Nemesis, called the Planet X argument, has also been proposed by scientists. Like the "Death Star," this planet has yet to be discovered. Acting much like the star, Planet X is thought to have grazed the Oort Cloud and caused a flock of comets or asteroids to fall on the earth. Upon impact, comets or asteroids would begin a series of events that would lead to the destruction of most plant and animal life.

While other theories exist that blame volcanic eruptions or molecular clouds for the death of the dinosaur, evidence for an impact theory has been found.

✌️A Castastrophic Impact

The Alvarez Team (a group of scientists) believed that the high iridium content found in the layer of rocks from sixty-five million years ago is proof that something collided with the earth at that time and caused serious destruction. This rare element - iridium - is concentrated many more times in meteorites than it is in the crust of the earth. The iridium in the core of the earth is too deep to have surfaced on a global scale. And since iridium has been found in rock from England to New Zealand, it seems to support the idea that a huge asteroid or comet, rich in iridium, ten km in length, traveling about 100,000 kilometers an hour, collided with the earth. The results would have been huge craters and dense particles filling the atmosphere and blocking off the sun for almost a million years. While some plant and animal life survived, most was destroyed.

While none of the theories has so far been proved true, scientists are continuing to explore the unknown as they try to find the answers to the mysteries of the past. Their hope: to protect man from becoming an extinct species if another catastrophe like the one the dinosaurs experienced is to happen in the future. If man can find out what event destroyed the dinosaurs, perhaps he can save himself!

PLESIOSAUR

✌️ This marine reptile used its powerful limbs in an up and down motion similar to that of today's turtle, not like oars as was originally believed.

32